THE RIDE OF A LIFETIME!

The roller coaster car slowed, then rolled to a stop.

Ashley and I sat without moving for a moment, breathing hard, waiting for the dizziness to fade. I suddenly heard music floating softly over the night air.

"The park is closed," I reminded Ashley. "Who would be playing music now?"

"Let's check it out," she said.

We made our way through a gap in a wooden fence—and stepped into a bright, crowded scene.

But it all looked different. The park. The people. Everything.

"James—" Ashley cried, grabbing the sleeve of my T-shirt. "This isn't Kings Island. Where *are* we?"

THE
BEAST™

R·L·STINE

A MINSTREL® BOOK

PUBLISHED BY POCKET BOOKS

New York   London   Toronto   Sydney   Tokyo   Singapore

This book is a work of fiction. Names, characters, places, and incidents are products of the author's imagination or are used fictitiously. Any resemblance to actual events or locales or persons, living or dead, is entirely coincidental.

A MINSTREL PAPERBACK *ORIGINAL*

 A Minstrel Book published by
POCKET BOOKS, a division of Simon & Schuster Inc.
1230 Avenue of the Americas, New York, NY 10020

ISBN: 0-671-88055-1

First Minstrel Books printing June 1994

10 9 8 7 6 5 4 3 2 1

A MINSTREL BOOK and colophon are registered trademarks of Simon & Schuster Inc.

Cover art by Tim Jacobus

Printed in the U.S.A.

To Joe,
who seldom gets off the track

THE
BEAST™

1

I shut my eyes as a shrill scream escaped my throat.

Bouncing hard, I opened them in time to see the trees fly by in a jarring blur. "Whoa!" I was tossed forward as I roared straight down into darkness.

A sudden spin made me cry out again. The car tilted hard to the left and I slammed into my cousin, Ashley Franks. She was screaming, too. Her blond hair flew out wildly behind her head.

We swooped down once more, a sharp dip. I yelped in surprise as I felt myself fly up from the seat. The trees whirred by, shadowy in the dark night light. The car clattered noisily as it began to climb again.

"This is *great!*" I screamed to Ashley.

Her face was bright red. Her blue eyes were wide, staring up to the top of the track. She grinned at me and started to reply. But instead, she let out a startled *whoop* as our car plunged down.

Down, down with a deafening roar.

The wind battered my face. I gripped the bar tightly with both hands. Down, down—and into total darkness.

"Huh?"

A tunnel. We whirred through the tunnel, then back out into the dim light filtering through the dark, leafy trees. Then a jolting turn pushed me into Ashley again. My cousin was screaming too hard to notice.

Another tunnel. Another climb. Another swooping, roaring spin that made the car squeal.

And then we slowed to a stop.

Over my thudding heartbeat I could hear screams and laughter behind us. Ashley and I had been riding in the front car.

I turned to her. She was still breathing hard. Her hair was wild, standing almost straight up. She was trying to brush it down with both hands.

"You were right, James!" she exclaimed. "The Beast® is *awesome!*"

"It's the best! I told you!" I cried breathlessly. I climbed out of the roller coaster car onto the platform. "Hey—I'm dizzy!"

"You're always dizzy," Ashley teased, following me out. She staggered for a few steps, then grabbed my shoulder. She laughed. "Whoa! I'm a little dizzy, too, I guess."

We staggered off the platform and followed the exit path. I turned back to stare at the enormous roller coaster, the wooden tracks rising up darker even than the night sky.

My heart was still racing. As Ashley and I walked, we were surrounded by laughing, shouting voices. "I—I thought the ride was over," Ashley said, still trying to untangle her hair. "But then we started to climb again."

"That has to be the longest roller coaster ride anywhere!" I exclaimed. "Other roller coasters last only a minute or two. But this one takes over four minutes!"

I'm an expert on roller coasters. I ride them whenever I can. And I never ride just once. I always go back and ride again and again.

The third time is usually the best. By that time, your screaming muscles are limbered up and you can howl like a pro all the way.

I'd been to Paramount's Kings Island twice before. And I had ridden The Beast at least half a dozen times. But this was Ashley's first time.

She's twelve and I'm twelve, but I think I look older. She's about four inches shorter than me, even with all that wild blond hair. She's skinny, too. I guess she's kind of pretty. She has great blue eyes and a nice smile.

People always tease me because I don't smile much. I've got dark brown hair and dark eyes, and I just look serious, that's all.

Ashley and I don't get to see each other very often. Our families live about three hundred miles apart. But when we do, we get along pretty well.

We like to tease each other and get on each other's case. Sometimes we play pretty mean tricks on each other. But I guess that's normal.

4

We stopped at a food stand and bought sodas. All that screaming can make you thirsty.

After gulping down half her cup of soda, Ashley glanced up at the dark sky. A pale half-moon had risen above the trees. "It's getting pretty late," she said. "Past your bedtime, James."

"Ha-ha," I replied, rolling my eyes.

She took another long gulp from her cup. Some of it trickled onto the front of her sleeveless blue T-shirt, but she didn't notice. She pushed her hair off her forehead with her free hand.

"What do you want to do now?" I asked. We had been at the park since early afternoon. We had already been on most of the other roller coasters.

"Let's ride The Beast again!" Ashley cried. Her eyes lit up as an excited grin crossed her face. "Come on!"

"The line is pretty long," I told her, motioning to it. I glanced at my watch. "And the park is going to close soon."

"Come on!" she cried, not listening to me. She tugged at the sleeve of my T-shirt. "Hurry!"

I pulled back. "No. Really. There isn't time, Ashley," I insisted.

"Please! Let's just try—okay?" she begged, tugging at me again. "Let's get in line again. Please?"

"Well . . . okay," I agreed.

And that was when all the trouble began.

2

Ashley and I jogged side by side to the end of the line. It stretched along a low wall in front of a line of trees. We were breathing hard by the time we got there.

Up ahead, we could hear the clatter of roller coaster cars and we could hear kids screaming their heads off. But we couldn't see them. The Beast stretches off into the woods. It's almost entirely hidden from view.

We stepped up behind two teenage boys. They both had long black hair. One of them wore a Cincinnati Reds cap. The one with the cap shoved the other one playfully against the wall. Then they both laughed.

A blue-uniformed guard stepped up suddenly behind Ashley and me. She set down a sign that said LINE CLOSED.

"We just made it!" Ashley cried happily. "We're the last ones!"

I glanced at my watch. I was a little worried about the time. I was supposed to call my mom when we were ready to be picked up.

But we were so busy riding all the roller coasters, I'd completely forgotten about calling. We'll have to phone her as soon as the ride is over, I told myself.

A cool breeze blew over us. I could hear high-pitched screams coming from the roller coaster up ahead.

"This is great!" Ashley cried. "I can't believe we're the very last ones in line!"

"Yeah. We just made it," I said.

The two guys ahead of us were goofing around. "Hey, Gary, give me my hat!"

"Who's going to make me?"

They started wrestling for the hat, laughing and shoving each other. The one named Gary bumped Ashley hard.

"Hey—" she cried out angrily.

"Sorry," he said, grinning at her. He pointed to his friend. "Ernie pushed me."

Ernie grabbed the Reds cap from Gary and pulled it over his dark hair. "You ever ride The Beast before?" he asked Ashley.

"Sure. About a hundred times," Ashley lied.

"You ever sit in the front seat?" Gary asked.

"Lots of times," Ashley told him.

"Were you scared?" Gary asked, grinning at me.

"No way!" I told him.

"You know, The Beast is haunted," Ernie said, adjusting his cap. His grin faded.

"Huh?" I stared back at him, trying to get the joke.

"Really," he insisted. "It's haunted."

"Everyone knows that," his friend chimed in.

"Give us a break," Ashley said, rolling her eyes.

"It was on the news," Gary told her. "On TV. I saw it."

"There's a ghost," Ernie said. "Late at night after the park is closed, he rides The Beast. Again and again."

"Oh, sure," I replied sarcastically. "Hey, we're not little kids, you know!"

9

R. L. STINE

"I'm not joking," Ernie said, his expression serious.

"It was on the news. Really," Gary added. "The ghost rides late at night. The security guards—they hear the clatter of the wheels. But when they run to check it out, none of the cars has moved."

"It's a total mystery," Ernie said, adjusting his cap again.

"No way!" I cried. "There's no ghost—"

But at that moment I felt icy fingers close around the back of my neck.

3

I let out a frightened yelp before I realized that Ashley had grabbed the back of my neck.

Everyone laughed.

Ashley laughed hardest of all. She thought it was a real riot.

"How'd you get such cold hands?" I demanded angrily.

She held up her cold cup of soda. "Gotcha!" she cried.

She could be a real pain sometimes. I could feel myself blushing. Luckily, the line had started to move, and the two teenage guys turned away.

"Do you think there's really a ghost that rides The Beast?" Ashley whispered as we followed the line forward.

"Of course not," I replied angrily. "Do you think there's really a tooth fairy?"

"You mean there *isn't?*" she cried, acting startled. "Then how do those quarters get under my pillow when I lose a tooth?"

She laughed, but her expression quickly became serious. "Those two boys believe in the ghost," she whispered. "They weren't kidding."

"There's no ghost," I insisted.

"But they saw it on the news," she replied.

We stepped onto the platform. The breeze felt cool and damp. I could still feel Ashley's cold fingers on the back of my neck. I shivered.

I glanced at my watch again. Nearly eleven o'clock. I had promised my mom I would call before ten. How could I have forgotten?

"We didn't call. Everyone will be furious," I muttered.

"Don't be such a nervous nut," Ashley replied.

"I'm not a nervous nut," I insisted. "Don't call me a nervous nut."

"You're a nervous nut," she repeated.

I tugged her blond hair hard.

She punched my shoulder.

I grabbed two of her fingers and stretched them till they cracked.

She punched me harder.

Luckily the line moved forward before we got out of control.

A few minutes later we were eagerly scrambling into a car. We were the last ones on The Beast. This time we were in the middle row of the last car.

When we were all on board, the heavy car began to roll. Up, up the steep track.

I knew what was ahead. I knew what would happen as soon as we reached the top.

And I couldn't wait.

I took a deep breath and prepared to start screaming.

The ride was even more awesome the second time. We swooped and swirled through the dark trees. The tunnels whirred around us. Then we climbed into the purple sky—and back down into the woods.

I felt as if I were on some kind of spaceship, hurtling into darkest space.

13

Suddenly I couldn't hear the screams and happy cries of the others. I couldn't see Ashley beside me or the kids in the seat in front of us.

I was in my own world.

A world of whirling shadows. A world of speed and wind.

When the car jolted to a stop, I groaned in disappointment. I didn't want the ride to end. I wanted to keep flying, soaring through the trees, the cold wind rushing against my face.

I just sat there for a long while with my eyes shut.

Even though we had stopped, I could still feel the movement of the car, still feel the jarring turns, the swooping slides, the steep climbs.

I don't know how long I sat there. Probably just a few seconds. Maybe it was close to a minute.

Then I opened my eyes and climbed out. "Wasn't that *excellent?*" I turned to ask Ashley. "Wasn't that the best?"

I gasped when I realized she was *gone!*

4

"Ashley?"

I gazed up and down the platform.

People were hurrying to the exit, laughing and shouting. I didn't see her anywhere.

"Ashley?"

I turned back to the roller coaster car. Was she still there?

No.

Had she somehow managed to climb out on the other side of the car? No. That was impossible.

So where was she?

"Ashley?" I cupped my hands around my

mouth and shouted. My voice came out kind of trembly. I was still shaky from the ride.

She must have hurried to the exit, I decided. She would be waiting for me outside the gate.

My heart was still pounding and my knees were a little wobbly as I started jogging down the platform and out of the roller coaster.

My shadow stretched long and dark in front of me as I ran. The overhead lights flickered on and off. A woman's voice suddenly blared out from a nearby loudspeaker. "Paramount's Kings Island is now closed," she announced. "Please make your way to the front exit."

The announcement repeated a few times as the overhead lights continued to signal everyone to leave.

"Ashley?" I stopped in front of The Beast's exit, searching the shadows for her.

No sign of her.

I made my way past a T-shirt and souvenir stand, closed now for the night. Several yards up ahead, I saw Gary and Ernie, bumping each other as they made their way toward the front of the park.

I stopped and made a full circle, turning

slowly, studying each person I saw, searching for Ashley.

But she had totally disappeared.

"I don't believe this," I muttered out loud.

How could she do this to me? If this is some kind of joke, I thought, I'll pound her! I really will!

The lights flickered one last time, then remained dimmed. The announcement about the park being closed repeated a few more times.

We've got to get out of here, I told myself.

But where was Ashley? Where?

The ghost got her!

That thought popped into my head.

The ghost that haunts The Beast grabbed her during the ride!

I was so angry at Ashley, I almost wished it were true. But of course, it was a stupid thought.

Without realizing it, I had started to walk toward the front of the park. I found myself in a large group of people who had just come off The Vortex, the roller coaster next to The Beast.

The Vortex was a wild ride. It swirled you

upside down about six times. At least, I *think* it was six times. After a few spins I lost count.

Ashley and I had ridden The Vortex right after dinner. Not exactly the best timing. But our stomachs survived.

Except maybe the ride had scrambled Ashley's brain! I thought angrily. What else could explain her disappearing like this?

I'll wait for her at the front gate, I decided. She's bound to show up there sooner or later.

Sooner, I hoped.

I remembered there was a row of pay phones near the ticket booths. Maybe that was where Ashley had headed. I could call my mom from there.

I made my way down International Street, the broad walkway at the front of the park. The long reflecting pond in the center of the street lay dark and still. The fountains that sent up tall geysers of water during the day had all been turned off.

How could she just disappear? I asked myself. I was growing angrier and angrier.

What is her problem?

It felt strange walking through the dim light, stepping through shifting shadows. The enormous park had been so bright and noisy. Now it was nearly dark and empty.

On the other side of the gate, car headlights rolled past, casting bright spotlights on the hundreds of people heading to their cars.

I jogged to the row of telephones, my heart pounding. My eyes searched the shadows, darting rapidly over the crowd.

No sign of my cousin.

I had a heavy feeling in the pit of my stomach. Like a rock holding me down. I stopped a few yards from the pay phones.

I took a deep breath and held it, waiting for the heavy feeling to fade away.

"Ashley—where are you?" I murmured.

Why wasn't she waiting at the gate for me? Why wasn't she standing by the pay phones?

Taking another deep breath, I watched the last stragglers head out to the parking lot. The park grew even more silent. The loudest sounds were the hum of car engines as they pulled away.

The heavy feeling in my stomach didn't go away. I knew it wouldn't. It was worry. I always got that heavy feeling when I was worried. Really worried.

Something must have happened to Ashley.

Something bad.

She wouldn't just disappear. Even Ashley wouldn't play a dumb joke like that.

A cold shiver ran down my back.

Yes, I decided, trying to force back my panic. Something has happened to Ashley.

But what?

5

All kinds of crazy thoughts roared into my head. Without realizing it, I started back into the park.

I hurried past the long reflecting pool. A tall replica of the Eiffel Tower stood at the far end, black against the starless purple sky.

The electric lights had all been dimmed. A damp mist had lowered over the park. I felt as if I were moving through a cloud.

It was like a dream. Swirling shadows in the thickening mist. Dim yellow light casting looming, eerie forms.

No one in sight.

The huge park stretched out on all sides of me. Deserted. The stores and restaurants dark and empty.

"Ashley?" Her name escaped from my throat. My voice came out shaky and high.

This *is* a dream, I told myself.

This *has* to be a dream. And I'm going to wake up and find that I haven't really lost my cousin.

I shook my head hard, trying to shake the nightmare away.

But it wasn't a dream.

I had run halfway to the tall, dark tower before I stopped.

Why was I doing this? Where did I think I was going?

My heart was thudding in my chest. The heavy rock in my stomach grew even heavier.

I have to get back to the front gate, I told myself. I have to call home. I have to—

"Hey—James!"

I heard the familiar voice. But staring into the heavy mist, I saw no one.

"James!"

I spun around and was surprised to see Ashley come running from the side of a darkened pastry shop. In the pale light through the heavy fog, she looked like a ghost, her bare arms white, her blond hair fanned out behind her.

She stopped a few feet in front of me, breathing hard. "Where *were* you?" she cried breathlessly.

"Huh?" My mouth dropped open.

"Where *were* you?" she repeated angrily.

"Where were *you?*" I cried shrilly. "I got off the roller coaster—and you were gone!"

"No. *You* were gone!" she insisted. She shoved me hard with both hands. "What a jerk!"

"You're the jerk!" I cried, stumbling backward. I was so angry, I moved forward to shove her back. Then all at once I realized how funny the whole thing was.

"I was searching for you, and you were searching for me!" I exclaimed, laughing.

"It's not funny!" Ashley cried. "I got off The Beast and started for the exit. I glanced back to make sure you weren't there. So I thought you'd gotten ahead of me. I started running to catch up to you. But—but . . ." Her voice trailed off. She took a deep breath.

"I wasn't ahead of you. I was behind you," I explained.

"I got turned around. I thought I was heading toward the front gate," Ashley continued. "But I ended up at The Vortex. By the time I got back in the right direction—"

"Let's just get out of here!" I cried.

We began running to the main gate, our sneakers thudding on the pavement.

"The park is so *weird* looking!" Ashley cried as we ran.

She was right. The fog had grown even heavier, thicker. The dimmed light from overhead landed at strange angles. It got tangled in the mist, made the ground appear to shimmer and smoke.

"It—it's really hard to see," I called to her. I was staring straight ahead but couldn't see the front gates through the fog. Glancing down, I saw that my shadow had completely disappeared.

We moved quickly, silently, through the fog. Past the dark and still reflecting pool.

We ran faster when the front gates came into view.

The heaviness in my stomach had vanished, replaced by a sharp ache in my side as I ran.

"Finally!" Ashley cried.

She reached the exit first. She gripped the bars of the gate and pulled.

It didn't budge.

She pulled again. Then she tried pushing.

When she turned back to me, her expression revealed her panic. "James—we're locked in!" Ashley cried.

6

The next gate was locked, too. And so was the next.

We ran from gate to gate, trying to find one unlocked. But the entire row of metal exit gates was locked.

The vast parking lot had become empty and dark. Far in the distance I could just see the red taillights of the last cars.

"Hey—let us out!" Ashley cried.

But there was no one to hear her.

The fog closed in on us, swirled around us, blanketed us in darkness. I knew there had to be security guards somewhere nearby. But the fog had become so thick, it was hard to see even a few feet in any direction.

Ashley stepped close beside me. Her hair fell in tangles over her forehead. She rubbed her bare arms, trying to warm them in the wet, cold fog.

"Your mom is going to have a cow!" she cried unhappily.

My mom! Of course!

In all the confusion I had forgotten about calling. The pay phones were right behind us. All we had to do was call my mom and she'd come rescue us.

No problem.

"The phones! Come on!" I cried. I turned and started to make my way through the swirling fog toward the phones. "Have you got a quarter?" I called back to her.

She searched the pockets of her baggy shorts. "Yeah. Here."

I took the quarter from her and stepped up to the phone booth. I lifted the receiver and started to drop the quarter in the slot.

Suddenly a hand grabbed my wrist.

"Don't!" Ashley said softly.

I spun around, startled. "What's your problem?" I demanded.

"Don't call," Ashley repeated, her eyes lighting up excitedly. She still hadn't let go of my wrist.

"Huh? What are you talking about?" I asked shrilly. "You want to get out of here—don't you?"

She shook her head. A mischievous grin spread over her face. "No," she whispered.

Then she grabbed the quarter out of my fingers. "No."

I held out my hand. "Ashley—give me back the quarter. You're not funny."

Grinning at me, she backed away. She dropped the coin back into the pocket of her shorts. "Let's stay, James," she pleaded. "Let's stay in the park all night."

I gaped at her. My mouth dropped open. "Huh? Are you for real?"

"Come on—it'll be cool!" she exclaimed. She tried to tug me away from the phones. But I pulled out of her grasp.

"We'll get caught," I told her. "We'll get into big trouble."

"We'll hide," she replied. "It'll be a real adventure."

"I don't like adventure," I confessed. "There

are security guards all over this place. We'll get caught, Ashley. Give me the quarter."

I reached out for it. But she backed away, shaking her head, flashing me that devilish grin.

What a pain.

"You're crazy," I told her.

"You're no fun," she replied.

"It's cold and foggy. It's creepy here at night," I said. "What's the fun part?"

"I want to see the ghost," she confessed.

So *that* was it!

"Ashley, you didn't believe that dumb story about some ghost riding The Beast at night. Those guys were just goofing," I told her.

"No, they weren't. They were serious," she insisted.

"Ashley, there's no ghost," I said firmly. "Now, if you won't give me the quarter, I'll call home collect." I started back toward the phones.

"Prove there's no ghost," she called after me.

I turned around. "What do you mean— *prove* it?"

"Prove it," she repeated, tossing her hair

back over her shoulders. "Let's go watch. Let's see if anything happens."

"Ashley!" I moaned. "Don't be a jerk."

"I'll bet you ten dollars," she said.

"Huh?" She caught me off guard. "You'll bet me ten dollars *what?*"

"That the ghost comes out," she replied, her eyes wide, challenging me. "If it doesn't appear, I'll pay you ten dollars."

It was a stupid bribe. But Ashley knew that I can never turn down a bet. It's a real weakness.

I once had to stand on my head and whistle "Oh, Susannah" on the beach in front of a crowd of girls for ten minutes just because I bet my older brother that I could. It was so embarrassing! You'd think I'd learn my lesson.

But I never did.

"Okay, it's a bet," I told Ashley. I couldn't believe I was agreeing. I knew we could get into major trouble if a security guard found us. And what about our parents?

Ashley had that all figured out. She reached into her pocket and pulled out the quarter. "Here. Call your mom and tell her we're staying at one of your friend's houses tonight. Tell her we met him here and his parents drove us home," she said, tossing me the quarter.

I missed, and it hit the ground. I bent down and grabbed it quickly, before it rolled away in the heavy darkness.

"Clever," I said. "Very clever."

Why was I going along with this? Just to win ten dollars? I knew it was a horrible idea. I had that heavy feeling in my stomach again.

Why was I going to spend the night in a foggy park, hanging out, hiding, waiting for a ghost to ride The Beast?

Because of a ten-dollar bet?

I guess I was doing it so Ashley wouldn't call me a jerk again.

I mean, that's a pretty good reason—isn't it?

I made my call. It seemed to go okay. My mom was annoyed that we didn't call when we were supposed to, but she was tired and didn't ask too many questions.

Then, huddling close, we made our way through the dimly lit park toward the woods that hid The Beast.

The fog swirled around us. The soft light got caught up in the fog and barely made it to the ground.

I gazed around at the dark shops and restaurants, the empty game booths, closed and silent. It was all so eerie. And the heavy fog made it even more dreamlike and unreal.

"This is creepy," I whispered. "Too creepy."

"It's exciting," Ashley corrected me. "It's the perfect night for a ghost to come out, don't you think?"

"Yeah. Perfect," I muttered.

I didn't believe in ghosts. And I didn't think Ashley did either.

But Ashley believed in adventure. In a big way.

I always thought it was just a stage she was going through. But I guess she hadn't made it through it yet.

We were passing a frozen lemonade stand, its window closed, when we heard footsteps. Nearby.

"Quick—over here!" Ashley whispered.

She grabbed my arm and pulled me behind a tall shrub beside the lemonade stand.

But she was too late.

A blue-uniformed security guard moved quickly out of the fog. He was in front of us before I could duck behind the shrub.

"Hey—caught you!" he shouted.

7

With a silent gasp I dropped to my knees behind the shrub. Ashley huddled beside me.

The security guard laughed as he stepped forward.

We're in major trouble now, I thought.

Then I heard another laugh.

"Caught you," the guard repeated.

Peering over the top of the bush, I saw *two* blue-uniformed guards, both tall and powerful looking.

The guard stepped right in front of Ashley and me to greet his friend.

"Just taking a breather," the second guard said. "Some fog, huh?"

"Yeah. My flashlight hardly cuts through it," the first man replied. "Weird."

Behind the pine shrub, Ashley and I grinned at each other. We realized the guard hadn't even seen us. I had been holding my breath the whole time. Now I let it out in a long *whoosh* and started breathing normally again.

"Where are you tonight?" the first guard asked.

"Rivertown," his friend replied. "It'll be a quiet night."

They chatted for a little while longer. I couldn't hear what they were saying.

I practically jumped out of the bush when Ashley tapped my shoulder. I spun around angrily. Why did she have to scare me like that?

"Come on," she whispered. "We'll be late."

Late? Late for what?

I shook my head and pointed to the two guards, who were still chatting away.

"They won't see us," Ashley whispered. "It's too foggy and dark." She yanked on my arm so hard, she nearly knocked me over.

"Stop pulling me," I protested in a loud whisper. But I obediently climbed to my feet. Ducking low, I began to follow her.

A row of low bushes and trees followed the path. We stayed behind them as we tiptoed away.

I could still hear the two guards talking, somewhere behind us now.

A sudden gust of wind made the bushes shiver. My heart was pounding in my chest. My legs felt as if they each weighed a thousand pounds.

My sneakers sank into the wet grass. The bushes shook again. The trees began to whisper. Wisps of fog swirled just above our heads.

"Hurry," Ashley urged a few yards ahead of me.

I began to feel a little better, a little more relaxed.

That had been a close call. But we were getting away from the guards.

Then I tripped over something hard—a low metal fence.

I cried out in surprise as I fell out onto the pavement.

The fence clattered loudly beneath me.

I landed hard on my elbows and knees.

"Hey!" Both guards shouted at once.

I frantically tried to scramble to my feet. But this time I knew we really were caught.

8

I struggled to my feet.

Both knees throbbed with pain as I started to run. Stumbling, staggering forward.

I could hear the startled shouts of the guards close behind me. White beams of light from their flashlights bobbed along the path.

I dived over a clump of tall flowers and started running across the grass. Through the fog I caught glimpses of Ashley up ahead, running, running at full speed, her arms thrashing the air as she moved, almost as if she were swimming through the misty darkness.

"Hey—stop!" The guard's shout rang out from the path.

The sharp voice cut through me like a saw's blade. I uttered a frightened gasp. And somehow kept running.

My sneakers squished over the soft ground.

I could hear the two guards close behind, their flashlights darting wildly over the bushes as they ran.

Suddenly I found myself running between tall trees. We were in the woods now. I followed the crunch of Ashley's sneakers somewhere up ahead.

The fog grew thicker, wetter. Beads of cold water ran down my face.

I was gasping for breath. I tried to ignore the sharp pain in my side. But it had forced me to slow down.

Ashley had stopped. I caught up with her. She had her back against a tree. She was bent forward, hands pressed on her knees, trying to catch her breath.

I stopped in front of her and rubbed my sides, trying to rub the pain away.

"Nice move, ace," she whispered, making a face at me.

"I couldn't help it. I tripped," I whispered back.

We both listened hard.

We couldn't hear the guards.

Off to the right, I could see two flickering beams of light. The light appeared to be moving in the other direction.

"I—I think we lost them," I whispered. My throat felt as dry as cotton. I could barely choke out the words.

We stood watching the lights until they disappeared in the darkness. A cold chill ran down my back. My sneakers were soaked. The bottoms of my jeans were wet, too.

"What are we doing here?" I asked Ashley bitterly.

"We have a bet—remember?" she replied.

She stepped away from the tree. "Come on. This is fun."

"Fun? Fun?" I cried, hurrying to keep up with her as she slipped quickly through the trees. "So far, Ashley, I'm not having fun."

A few minutes later the trees ended and we found ourselves in a flat clearing. I gazed around, struggling to see through the fog. The sky seemed to grow darker. The only sound was the chirping of crickets in the trees.

"Now we're really lost," I grumbled, shoving my hands into my jeans pockets.

"No, we're not," Ashley replied quietly.

"Huh? Then, where are we?" I demanded.

"Look," she said. She pointed straight ahead.

I suddenly realized it wasn't the black sky I'd been staring at. It was The Beast. It rose up in front of us, blacker than the night.

The roller coaster hovered over the woods like an enormous creature ready to pounce.

Ashley and I stood staring up at the dark tracks for a long time. Black against the fog-covered sky, the tracks stretched up like a mountain, then curved away.

"Cool," Ashley murmured. "Let's go."

We crossed the clearing, ducked through an opening in a wood fence, and stepped onto the pavement. Tall spotlights overhead cast dim light over the area. I realized we were standing where the lines formed for The Beast.

Staying in the shadow of the fence, we searched for security guards.

None around.

Then we went running up the ramp onto the platform.

"This is totally weird!" I exclaimed. It had

been so crowded an hour earlier, filled with laughing, shouting, screaming people. And now it stood before us, so empty and silent.

"Yeah. Weird," Ashley agreed. Her eyes flashed excitedly.

We followed the platform to the front, our eyes searching the empty tracks.

The roller coaster cars stood at the far end. They looked bigger without people in them.

A gust of wind rolled over the platform, whistling through the tracks. I heard a soft flapping sound overhead.

A bat?

I glanced up to the platform roof. But it was too dark to see.

"I'll bet we're the only kids ever to see The Beast like this," Ashley said softly. She walked over to the first car and climbed inside.

"Ashley—what do you think you're doing?" I cried in alarm.

"If we're going to wait for the ghost, we might as well get comfortable," she replied. She scooted over, making room for me. "Come on, James." She patted the seat.

"No thanks," I told her, staying back from the tracks. "I'd rather stand."

"Come on. Sit down," she urged. "We can pretend we're roaring over the tracks."

"I don't like to pretend," I insisted. "I'm too old to pretend."

I heard the flapping sound overhead again. It had to be a bat. With a shudder, I let my eyes follow the dark tracks. They rolled out straight for a while before beginning their steep climb.

"When do you think the ghost will come out?" Ashley asked, leaning over the safety bar.

"There's no ghost," I muttered for the hundredth time. "This is one bet I'm going to win."

"We'll see," Ashley replied. "You sure you don't want to sit down?"

I started to reply, but stopped when I heard the loud clanking sound.

The clanking grew louder. The tracks groaned.

"Hey!" Ashley cried out.

I gaped, frozen with horror as the roller coaster cars started to move!

"Help me!" Ashley called from the front of the first car. "James—help!"

9

"Oh, no!"

I uttered a choked cry as I stared at the cars clanking over the tracks.

The cars were starting to pick up speed. In a few seconds they would make it past the platform.

And so would Ashley.

I saw that she had climbed to her feet and was struggling to climb out.

"James—help!"

Forgetting my fear, I started to run after her, my sneakers slapping the concrete platform.

The empty cars clattered noisily as they bounced over the tracks.

Could I get to her in time?

A few feet from the platform edge, I reached out with both hands.

She grabbed them.

I tugged—and pulled her from the car as it rolled out of sight.

We staggered back over the platform, breathing hard.

I could hear the empty cars making their climb up the steep first hill of the tracks.

"Are you okay?" I asked Ashley.

Her hair was wild around her face. She tugged it back with both hands. "I—I couldn't get out," she stammered. "My foot was caught and—"

We both could hear the empty cars rolling above us on the dark tracks. The sound of the clattering wheels echoed eerily off the empty platform.

"Why did the cars start moving?" Ashley asked. "There's no one around. This is so creepy, James."

I looked for the usual excited gleam in her eye. But this time I saw only fear.

THE BEAST

Hearing another sound, a loud *thunk,* we turned back to the far end of the platform.

And there, through the shadowy light, dancing in the billowing curtain of fog, we saw a figure bent over the controls.

The ghost?

10

Ashley grabbed my arm. Her hand was as cold as ice.

Staring across the long, mist-covered platform, we saw him. Even in the dim light we could make him out clearly, his white beard, his long white hair hanging down over his shirt collar.

He wore big, old-fashioned–looking overalls over a black, long-sleeved sweater. His hands were on the control levers. His head was lowered in concentration.

He hadn't seen us.

Could he see us? I suddenly wondered.

I've read a lot of science-fiction stories. If he

were a ghost from another dimension, I knew he might not be able to see us or communicate with us.

He might live in a totally different world.

But then, how did he get the roller coaster cars to run? I asked myself.

Ashley was still gripping my arm. I had to pull her hand away. She was squeezing so hard, she was hurting me.

"I—I think I just won my bet," she stammered, staring straight at the white-bearded ghost.

"Let's get out of here!" I whispered.

I turned to start down the ramp. But Ashley didn't follow.

I glanced back to see her frozen in place, her hands tensed into tight fists, her eyes wide with fright.

"Ashley—come on!" I called in a loud whisper.

And then I saw the ghost raise his eyes from the controls.

He saw Ashley first. Then me.

He stood up quickly, dropping his hands from the levers. He slid out from behind the control box and took a step toward us.

"Come here!" he boomed.

11

I swallowed hard. "Ashley—let's go!" I cried.

She didn't move. She stared straight ahead at the white-haired ghost as if she were hypnotized or something.

"Come here," he repeated in his deep, booming voice. "Both of you." The command echoed off the platform walls.

I hesitated at the top of the ramp. I wanted to run, but knew I couldn't leave Ashley alone.

"Ashley, please!" I pleaded.

But I saw her begin to move toward the ghost.

"Come over here," the ghost commanded again, waving both hands.

I took a deep breath and followed Ashley. A loud clatter startled us both. It took me a short while to see that it was the empty roller-coaster cars returning from their trip.

"How did you kids get in here?" the ghost asked. His body shimmered in the fog as if he were part of the mist.

As I edged closer, I could see his steel-gray eyes, almost silver. They peered at us sharply beneath heavy white eyebrows.

He was an old man, but powerfully built. He stood straight and tall like a much younger person. He had a broad chest beneath the overall bib, and big, strong-looking hands.

He was solid. Too solid to be a ghost, I told myself.

Ashley and I were only a few feet from him now. A gust of wind made his long white hair flutter. The wind whistled eerily down the dark tracks.

"We—we accidentally got locked in the park," Ashley told him.

He stared at her suspiciously. Then he turned his strange gray eyes on me. "What's your name, son?"

"James Dickson," I replied quickly. I pointed to Ashley. "She's my cousin. Ashley Franks."

"Pleased to meet you," the old man said. "I'm P. D. Walters." He stretched out his hand to shake with each of us.

His hand was warm and dry. It didn't feel like a ghost hand.

I was beginning to think that maybe Ashley hadn't won the bet after all.

"What does the P.D. stand for?" Ashley asked, studying the old man's face.

"Pretty Dumb!" he joked. He let out a bellowing laugh that made his massive chest heave up and down. "At least, that's what most folks say."

Then, suddenly, all the humor left his face. His gray eyes lost their sparkle, grew dull and thoughtful. He rubbed the heavy white beard. "You kids are going to get caught," he murmured.

Was it a threat or a warning? I couldn't tell.

"What do you do here?" Ashley asked, ignoring his comment.

"Test the cars," he replied, pointing to the train of empty roller coaster cars.

"At night?" Ashley asked.

P.D. nodded. "At night."

"You mean you work here?" I blurted out. My voice sounded strange. Tight and shrill.

"You might say that," P.D. answered.

"Have you ever seen a ghost here?" Ashley demanded suddenly.

P.D. let out another bellowing laugh. Then he made his way back behind the controls.

He didn't answer Ashley's question, I realized.

"So you work here every night?" Ashley asked, stepping up in front of the control panel.

"Just about," P.D. told her. He rested his hands on the two long metal levers that stuck up from the electronic box.

He cleared his throat, then raised his eyes to hers. "I've been coming here for over sixty years," he said. Something in his voice sounded sad to me.

Then I remembered something. "Whoa! Wait a minute," I said. "Kings Island hasn't been here for sixty years."

"I know," P.D. replied softly. His eyes dimmed. He frowned. "It's sort of a long, sad story."

"Tell us!" Ashley insisted eagerly.

P.D. leaned his bulky weight against the platform wall. He motioned for us to come closer. Ashley and I stepped up to the control box.

He scratched his white beard slowly, staring first at Ashley, then at me, as if trying to decide whether to tell his story or not.

He cleared his throat again, a low rumble that started deep in his chest. "Before Kings Island, there was another park on this same spot," P.D. began. "It was called Firelight Park. That's because the park was lit by thousands of burning torches."

"Wow!" Ashley exclaimed. "That must have been beautiful!"

P.D. nodded solemnly. His eyes watered over. His expression remained sad. "It was beautiful," he said softly. "When I was younger, much much younger, I thought it was the most beautiful spot on earth."

"And it was right here where we're standing?" I asked, shoving my hands deep into my jeans pockets.

The old man nodded. "Many years ago." The wind ruffled his hair. He gripped the control levers. "When I was young, I spent as much time as I could at Firelight Park. I loved the lights, the exciting rides, the carnival shows. I liked being part of the crowds, the happy crowds."

He sighed, a sad sigh. Then he shut his eyes and remained silent for a moment.

The fog seemed to circle around him in the dim light. His white hair and beard shimmered like wisps of cloud around his solemn, wrinkled face.

"Nothing beautiful lasts," he murmured softly, opening his gray eyes. "One horrible night it was all gone."

Ashley and I stared at him. His eyes became as dull as the fog. His broad shoulders slumped forward.

"What happened?" I asked.

"Tornado," P.D. muttered. "Came without warning. A violent tornado. It swept over the park. It toppled the torches, the thousands of torches. In minutes the entire park was ablaze."

He shook his head sadly, his eyes focused far away, remembering.

"People died," he continued. "Hundreds of people died that night. In minutes the park was gone. Gone forever."

I swallowed hard. "Were you there?" I asked. "Were you there the night of the tornado?"

P.D. nodded. "Oh, yes," he replied, sighing. "I was there. June 15, 1931. It isn't a date I shall ever forget."

Ashley and I exchanged glances. I was suddenly cold all over.

I tried to imagine another amusement park, in another time, over sixty years ago, on this very spot. A park filled with the light of thousands of flickering torches.

I tried to imagine how it could disappear forever in one swoop of a tornado.

But it was too frightening to think about.

P.D.'s voice broke through the chill air. "Now I work here at night," he said quietly, "testing The Beast."

Suddenly his expression changed. A thin smile formed on his lips, and his gray eyes lit up.

He pointed to the empty roller coaster cars. "Want a ride?"

"Huh?" Ashley and I hesitated.

"Maybe we should get going," I said.

"But it would be awesome!" Ashley exclaimed. "Riding The Beast at night through the fog. The only ones on the entire ride!"

"Go ahead. Climb in," P.D. urged. He raised his hands on the long control levers. "Go ahead. I'll give you a good ride."

"Ashley, I don't think we should," I pleaded. "I really think—"

I stopped when I saw the beams of yellow light moving toward us.

Flashlights. Flickering over the pavement, approaching the ramp. At least four or five of them.

Security guards.

"They—they've found us!" I stammered. "We're caught!"

P.D. pointed to the front car. "Quick! Jump in!" he cried. "Hurry!"

12

Ashley and I took off for the empty car.

I could see the flashlights darting closer. The yellow fog lights cut through the thick fog like lasers. Behind the lights I could see the shadowy figures of the guards.

I reached the cars first and dived into the front seat. With a breathless cry, Ashley scrambled in behind me.

"Hey, stop—" I heard a guard shout.

"Stop them!" another guard cried.

As the safety bar slammed down, I heard the pounding footsteps of the guards as they moved toward us.

But then the footsteps were drowned out by the clatter of wheels as our car pulled away.

We bumped along the track. Ashley and I bounced hard, gripping the safety bar with both hands.

Bright lights invaded my eyes, blinding me for a moment.

"There they are!" I heard a guard shout.

"Stop them! Stop the ride!" another guard cried.

The bright lights rolled over Ashley and me, and then disappeared.

"Whoa!" I shouted as the car tilted up, tossing me back against the seat.

"We're climbing!" Ashley cried. "This is *so cool!*"

Up, up we climbed through the darkness. I waited for my eyes to adjust. The yellow glare of the guards' flashlights lingered in my eyes.

The car creaked as it climbed, pressing us back against the seats. Gazing up, I saw nothing but fog blanketing the sky.

"We got away!" Ashley shouted happily. "James—we got away! This is totally awesome!"

We may have gotten away, but only for a few minutes. When the ride ended, the guards would be waiting for us on the platform.

I started to remind Ashley of this fact. But before I could get a word out, we reached the top of the steep hill—and the car went roaring straight down over the dark tracks.

"YAAAAIIIIIII!"

We both were screaming our heads off now.

It was the most amazing feeling. Plunging through the darkness. All alone. Just the two of us.

The car swung sharply and tilted hard, tossing us together. Then we bounced hard up a sharp incline. The car then straightened out and picked up speed.

I gripped the safety bar and stared out at the dark trees as they flashed by. Limbs poked out of the fog like bony black arms. Clouds of fog floated over the tracks.

The wind rushed at my face, cool and wet.

We both screamed as we plunged into a low tunnel. When we shot out, the fog appeared thicker. Heavier.

It seemed to wrap itself around us. Move with us.

We were part of the fog, swirling, floating, spinning around the tracks.

Ashley became a dim shadow beside me. We

were both dim shadows now. Shadows inside of shadows. Plunging through the wind, through the heavy, wet wind, through the pulsing, throbbing darkness.

The ride would end soon, I knew.

But I didn't know what awaited us. I couldn't know the terror at the end of the tracks.

13

The car slowed, then rolled to a stop.

Ashley and I sat without moving for a moment, breathing hard, waiting for the dizziness to fade.

I turned to the platform, expecting to see the bright flashlights and the dark figures behind the lights.

But the platform lay dark and empty.

"Hey—they're gone," I whispered.

"The guards? They're not here?" Ashley asked breathlessly.

We stood up and climbed out of the car. Ashley was pushing back her thick hair with both hands. My legs felt kind of wobbly, but my head was clear.

I gazed down the long, dark platform—and realized that the fog had disappeared.

"Hey!" I cried out, startled. "Ashley, look!" I pointed up to a sky full of twinkling stars.

"Huh?" She didn't catch on at first.

"How did the fog lift so fast?" I demanded. "A few seconds ago it was so thick, we couldn't see!"

Ashley shook her head. "I don't get it. Where's P.D.?"

I was so startled that no guards were waiting for us, so surprised to stare up into a clear sky that I had forgotten all about him.

I turned toward the control panel at the front of the platform. "P.D.?"

No one there. The control box stood in darkness.

Ashley and I gazed up and down the platform. We were the only ones there.

"Weird," she muttered.

I suddenly heard music. Very faint. Floating over the soft night air.

Ashley heard it, too. "It sounds like someone playing an organ," she said.

"The park is closed," I reminded her. "Who would be playing music now?"

"Let's check it out," she said.

We made our way off the platform and through the exit area. As we walked, the music grew louder.

Over the music I could suddenly hear voices. Laughter. Kids shouting.

"What's going *on?*" I cried.

We made our way through a narrow gap in a wooden fence—and stepped into a bright, crowded scene.

Flickering torches on tall poles marked both sides of a wide boardwalk. I saw a row of low game booths, brightly painted signs, food stands, long lines of people.

But it all looked different. It all was totally changed. The park. The people. Everything.

"James—" Ashley cried, grabbing the sleeve of my T-shirt. "This isn't Kings Island. It's weird. Where are we?"

She gripped my sleeve tighter as we both gaped in amazement.

"Where are we, James?" Ashley repeated shrilly. "Where *are* we?"

14

Our mouths open in surprise, we walked side by side, following the twin rows of torches. Past the game booths stood an old-fashioned carousel with pink and white horses spinning gracefully.

A high white building stood across from it. The sign over the wide entrance proclaimed ANGLUND'S WILD ANIMAL SHOW.

"Everyone is dressed so weird!" Ashley exclaimed.

I had to agree with her. I didn't see anyone in jeans. Everyone was *too* dressed up for an amusement park. Most of the men wore dark hats. A lot of them were in sports jackets and ties. Their pants were baggy, pleated in front.

Two boys ran past in long brown shorts and striped T-shirts. They had heavy leather shoes on their feet. No sneakers.

The women and girls all wore dresses or skirts. The dresses were solid colors or flower prints and had big shoulders. Most of the skirts came down nearly to the women's ankles.

"Wow. Look at those high-heeled shoes," Ashley exclaimed. "Who would wear high heels to an amusement park?"

"The hair styles are weird, too," I said. "It's like we stepped into an old black-and-white movie on TV."

My comment made us both stop and stare at each other.

I think we had the feeling that something very mysterious had just happened to us. And I think at that moment we both knew where we were.

"We—we're in Firelight Park," Ashley stammered, her eyes gazing all around.

"But—how?" I managed to choke out.

Ashley didn't reply. She was staring at the flickering torches that lined all the walkways.

"This is—impossible," she murmured finally. "Impossible."

We both shook our heads, staring at this strange park in disbelief.

How did we get here?

How would we get back to Kings Island?

Were we trapped here? Trapped here forever?

These frightening questions flashed through my mind.

"I feel scared and excited and curious and terrified all at the same time!" Ashley exclaimed.

I nodded. "Me, too," I choked out.

"What do we do now?" she asked.

Two teenage boys wearing big blue sport shirts buttoned up to the collar and wide brown pants pushed past us. I followed them with my eyes. They were hurrying to a tall building in front of us.

A long line had formed in front of the entrance to the building. A sign made of hundreds of red and blue light bulbs proclaimed RIDE THE SHOOT-THE-CHUTE!

"What is the Shoot-the-Chute?" Ashley demanded.

I shrugged. "Some kind of water ride, I'd guess."

I suddenly noticed that people were staring at us. Mostly they were staring at Ashley.

Because of her clothes, I guessed. She had to be the only girl in sight in Day-Glo orange shorts, a sleeveless T-shirt, and white high-tops.

People were staring at my pump sneakers, too. And I guess my faded jeans with holes at both knees and my Heavy Metal Headbangers T-shirt were a little out of place.

"I feel like some kind of freak," Ashley complained. "Why are they staring at me like that?"

"They're the ones who are dressed funny!" I cried.

"I don't like this," Ashley said, her voice trembling. "I really don't like this, James."

"Hey—you wanted an adventure, right?" I replied. I tried to sound cheerful. I was probably as frightened as Ashley. Maybe more frightened.

I watched her chin tremble and her eyes start to tear up. I didn't want her to lose it. So I forced myself to sound cheerful. Like I was having a good time. Not a care in the world.

"It's so hot," I said, wiping my forehead with one hand. "Let's get some ice cream."

I led the way to a small white cart with a green- and white-striped umbrella over it. A short, chubby man in a long white apron leaned over the cart. He had shiny slicked-down black hair and a thin black mustache.

He lifted himself off the cart as Ashley and I stepped up. "What'll it be?" he asked.

"Do you have frozen yogurt?" Ashley asked.

The man narrowed his eyes at her. "You're a little late for April Fool's Day, miss," he said.

"No. Really. Frozen yogurt," Ashley repeated.

The man frowned. "Why would anyone freeze yogurt?"

"Ashley," I whispered. "He doesn't have it." I turned back to the ice-cream man. He was staring at Ashley's outfit.

"Do you have rocky road?" I asked.

He rolled his eyes. "Another joker. You two are Abbott and Costello, huh?"

"I'll have praline ice cream," Ashley said.

The man's skinny little mustache twitched, as if it were about to jump off his face. He rubbed his chin with a chubby hand. "You two are funny. You should go on the radio. You dress funny, too. Where'd you get those costumes?"

"What flavors do you have?" I asked.

"Vanilla and chocolate, naturally," he said, rolling his dark eyes impatiently. "And I've got tutti-frutti."

"Tutti-*what?*" Ashley asked shrilly. "What's that?"

I could see the man was starting to get angry. And glancing behind us, I saw that a small crowd had gathered. Our strange clothing was attracting attention.

"We'll have two vanilla cones," I said quickly.

The man nodded, opened the lid on the white cart, and began scooping ice cream into two cones. I dug into my jeans pocket and felt a couple of dollar bills. I hoped it would be enough to pay for the cones.

"That'll be four cents," the man said, handing us two double-scoop cones.

"Ashley—a double-dip cone for two cents!" I cried in surprise.

Her mouth had dropped open in shock.

"Have you got it or not?" the man asked, hands at the waist of his apron.

I pulled a nickel from my pocket. "Keep the change," I told him. Big spender.

"Can you tell me what year this is?" Ashley asked suddenly.

The man's wormlike mustache twitched again. He narrowed his eyes at her. "What did you ask me?"

"What year is this?" Ashley repeated as if it were a perfectly normal question to be asking an ice-cream man at an amusement park.

The man didn't reply. He shook his head and muttered something about kids today. He gave us a weary little wave. "See you in the funny papers," he said, and turned away from us.

Ashley and I walked away, licking our enormous cones. The ice cream was really good, sweet and creamy.

As we walked, I noticed that people stared and pointed at us. "Funny costumes," I heard a woman say. "Are they in the circus show?"

"We've got to do something," Ashley whispered. She had a white ice-cream mustache over her mouth. The cones were very drippy.

"We've got to find P.D.," I said. "He'll know

what to do. And he'll probably know how to get us home."

"Don't say *probably*," Ashley said shrilly. "He's *got* to know how to get us home. He's *got* to!"

We wandered through the crowd, trying to ignore the stares and comments. The line had grown longer at the Shoot-the-Chute. We also passed a long line at a ride called Moon Rocket.

Peering into the entrance, I saw a long rocket ship, very old-fashioned looking, with dozens of little cars like little train cars. It looked more like a huge caterpillar than a rocket. It was wrapped around a circular track.

And when the cars were filled with passengers, the rocket spun around the track, faster and faster. The passengers squealed and shouted, even though they weren't going as fast as a roller coaster.

I guess they thought it was pretty fast though.

"Hey—James!" Ashley pulled me away from the entrance.

I spun around, trying to see what she was pointing at.

"It's P.D.!" she cried, starting across the crowded plaza.

Staring into the bright light of the tall torches, I saw him against a low fence. I recognized the long white hair and the baggy denim overalls.

"Hurry!" Ashley cried, pushing her way through the crowd.

She didn't have to tell me to hurry. I was just as eager to talk to P.D. as Ashley was.

Now maybe we'll find out what's going on here, I thought.

He's got to get us out of here. He's *got* to!

"Hey, P.D.!" Ashley called.

When he turned around, we both gasped.

15

"P.D.?" Ashley's voice sank.

The white-haired man spun around. His dark eyes glanced back at us through heavy black-rimmed glasses. He held a stubby black pipe in his teeth. No beard.

Ashley and I both saw at once that it wasn't P.D.

The man turned to his wife and pointed at us. I guessed he was commenting on our weird outfits.

Ashley sighed and shook her head.

"Keep searching," I said. "We'll find him."

We walked past a small square park. A

crowd had gathered in front of a white band-stand. On the low stage a quartet wearing straw hats and red- and white-striped shirts was singing a slow song.

"It's a barbershop quartet," Ashley said.

"Well, I could tell it wasn't a rap group!" I exclaimed sarcastically.

We stopped for a moment to search the crowd. No sign of P.D.

The four singers leaned close together. They were singing something about an old Kentucky home.

Ashley and I started walking again. A strong breeze came up, making the torch flames flutter. Our shadows grew longer.

We passed a small food stand selling Coney Island dogs. In the far distance I could see a Ferris wheel, dark against the purple sky.

The wind fluttered Ashley's hair. She didn't seem to notice. Her eyes were narrowed, searching for P.D.

An idea popped into my head. "Hey—I bet he's waiting for us back at The Beast," I said.

"Maybe," Ashley replied. The wind blew her hair over her forehead. She pushed it back with both hands.

"Which way is The Beast?" I asked. "I'm all turned around."

"Let's ask that guard," Ashley said.

Across the walkway, a guard in a blue uniform leaned against a narrow wooden booth. It looked like those photo-developing booths they have in malls, except it was painted blue.

We jogged over to him. "Which way is The Beast?" Ashley asked eagerly.

He stared back at us with cold brown eyes. He adjusted his blue cap as he studied us.

"Which way is The Beast?" Ashley repeated.

He frowned. "What's The Beast?"

"You know. The roller coaster," Ashley repeated impatiently.

"You mean the Shoot-the-Chute? It's over there." He pointed.

"No. It's called The Beast," I said. "It's back in the woods. But we lost our way and—"

"I see you lost your clothes, too," the guard said sternly.

"Can you tell us where The Beast is?" I asked.

He shook his head. "Try the wild animal show. They've got the only beasts I've ever heard of."

"But—but—" I stammered.

The guard narrowed his eyes at Ashley. "I'm sorry, miss. But I really can't allow you to walk around in your underwear like that."

Ashley's mouth dropped open. "Huh? My underwear?"

"An undershirt and shorts are not proper attire," the guard said. "Are your parents in the park?"

"No," Ashley muttered.

"Well, wait right here. I'll get someone to take you to the office. You can call them to come pick you up."

Ashley and I exchanged glances. "That would be a real long distance call!" Ashley told the guard.

The guard scowled. "I can't let you walk around like that. Just wait here."

"No way!" Ashley cried.

She wheeled around and started to run. I was a few steps behind her. But I stopped short, nearly colliding with a baby carriage.

"Stop! Stop right there!" I heard the guard scream.

He grabbed for me with both hands.

I ducked away. Fell. Landed hard on my

knees. My poor knees were having a rough night!

Glancing up, I saw Ashley running full speed through the startled people in the crowd.

I struggled to my feet. But the guard was right behind me.

I couldn't get away.

I was caught.

16

I stood up, swallowing hard, and waited for him to grab me.

But to my shock, he ran right past. "Stop her! Stop that girl!" he shouted.

I realized he wasn't interested in me. He only wanted to catch Ashley.

Shaking my head hard, as if shaking off a close call, I followed him. I saw Ashley turn a corner into a crowded area. I turned the corner too, but I lost sight of her.

People jammed the narrow walkway between two rows of brightly lit carnival booths. As I hurried past, searching for Ashley, I saw dart games, water balloon games, ring toss games.

"Win a Kewpie doll!" a man shouted through a megaphone. "Everyone's a winner! Win a Kewpie doll for your cutie!"

I had to slow to a walk. The crowd was too thick to run.

I couldn't see Ashley or the guard.

The wind whipped through the walkway. Women cried out and grabbed their skirts. Men held on to their hats. The flames of the tall torches flickered and bent.

A line had formed in front of a sideshow stage, blocking the street. I searched frantically for Ashley, but didn't see her.

I was starting to get that heavy feeling of dread in my stomach again. What if I couldn't find her?

On the sideshow platform, a man with a black mustache and oily, slicked-down black hair held a megaphone to his mouth. He wore a straw hat and a flashy, red- and black-striped sport jacket.

"See the two-headed boy!" he called into the megaphone, his shrill voice floating over the crowd. "It's real. It's all real, folks. The boy has two heads. You can count 'em for yourself!"

I pushed deeper into the crowd, searching for Ashley.

"Hurry, hurry! The show is about to begin. Two bits is all it takes, folks. Two bits to see the wonders of the known universe. See the amazing Elastic Woman! And her husband, the incredible Lobster Man! When she wraps him in her arms, she really wraps him, folks! But watch out—he pinches!"

Some people laughed. The crowd surged forward. I was forced to move along with it.

Another blast of wind made everyone reach for their hats.

Ducking my head, I pried myself free from the crowd. I turned the corner and was heading around the back of the sideshow—when someone grabbed my shoulder.

"Huh?" I spun around. "Ashley!"

"Quick—in here!" She pulled me to the back door of the sideshow building. Then she opened the door and slipped inside before I could protest.

We found ourselves in a steamy, dark room. A dim red lamp provided the only light.

I could hear low, murmuring voices nearby. And through the thin walls I could hear the carnival barker out front. "Hurry, hurry!" he was shouting. "The show is about to begin! You don't want to keep the Wild Man of Borneo waiting—do you, folks?"

My eyes were slowly adjusting to the dark. I turned and stared into Ashley's troubled face. "I—I think we lost that guard," she whispered.

"Then let's get out of here!" I urged.

She grabbed my arm. "But what are we going to do? That guard said there is no Beast here. He'd never heard of it. How are we going to find P.D.?"

"Maybe the guard is new here," I suggested. "Maybe he doesn't know his way around yet."

"Yeah. Sure." Ashley rolled her eyes. "Be serious, James. What are we going to do?"

"We'll just have to keep looking," I said. I pulled my arm free. "Hey—you're supposed to be the brave, adventurous one, remember?"

That made her smile. "Guess I forgot."

"Let's go find a map of the park," I suggested. "Then maybe we can—"

I stopped when I felt a cold, wet hand on my arm.

"Come on, let go, Ashley," I whispered.

She gaped at me. "I'm not touching you."

With a gasp, I turned to see a strange-looking teenage boy grinning at me. His face was shadowy and evil in the dim red light. His black eyes were wide, and his mouth appeared to be locked in its jagged grin.

"I'm the Jelly Boy," he said in a weird singsong. His cold, wet hand patted my arm, giving me chills.

"I'm the Jelly Boy," he repeated. "I'm a good boy. I'm the Jelly Boy."

17

He wrapped his cold, slimy hand around my hand. His arms and legs seemed soft and rubbery, like jelly. His grinning face was inches from mine. His breath smelled sour.

"I'm the Jelly Boy," he chanted. "I'm a good boy."

"Nice to meet you," I choked out. "My friend and I—we're leaving now."

I tried to slide my hand free. But he held on. His hand was so wet and cold, I had shivers running down my back.

"I'm the Jelly Boy. I'm the Jelly Boy." His grin never moved.

"Ashley—let's go!" I cried.

She started backing toward the door—then cried out.

I followed her gaze. A two-headed boy stepped out of the shadows into the red light. His left head was sort of tilted at an odd angle. The other head stood straight. All four eyes stared directly at us.

"Who are you?" the right head demanded in a surprisingly deep voice.

Before Ashley or I could reply, an enormous woman waddled into the room. She was so wide, she had trouble squeezing through the doorway. She wore a huge white dress, bigger than a camping tent. Her face was as round as a balloon, and she had at least twelve chins.

"What's going on?" she asked sharply.

"Uh—we're leaving," I managed to say in a trembling voice.

"No, you're not," the two-headed boy replied, moving quickly to block the door.

"You're staying with us," Jelly Boy whispered, bouncing on his rubbery, jellylike legs.

"You're staying with us forever," the two-headed boy said.

18

The strange, frightening weirdos started to close in on us.

I glanced at Ashley. She was tugging at her hair with both hands, her eyes wide with fright. "Let us *out!*" she shouted at them.

She turned to the door. But the two-headed boy was still blocking the way.

Suddenly a shrill voice boomed out from the front of the room. "Show time, guys. What's the delay?"

We all turned to stare at the carnival barker. He took off his straw hat and dropped it on a table beside his megaphone. "Let's not keep the fans waiting. Get a move on!" he ordered them.

"Wanda, get your beard on. Artie, straighten your head. It's falling off your shoulder. Come on, guys." His eyes went wide when he finally noticed Ashley and me.

"Hey—get those kids out of here!" he cried. "Are you guys scaring kids again? Don't you remember what happened in Dayton? Those poor kids will have nightmares for the rest of their lives."

The huge woman waddled away, pressing a beard up to her chin. The two-headed boy grumbled loudly as he struggled to straighten his fake head on his shoulder.

"Jelly, open the door. Get these kids out of here. Now!" the barker ordered.

"Okay, okay. I hear you!" the Jelly Boy muttered.

A few seconds later Ashley and I found ourselves back outside. The wind had picked up. It was ruffling the pennants on top of the game booths, making them rattle. The torches all down the walkway flickered low, almost blowing out.

"That was creepy," I said as we headed away from the carnival area.

"It was all a fake," Ashley murmured. Then she froze in place and her eyes went wide.

"James—run!" she cried.

I turned back to follow her frightened gaze.

Blue-uniformed park guards. There were four of them now.

They saw us—and were running after us.

We wanted to run. But we were standing in front of a solid brick wall.

19

"Quick—give me a boost!" Ashley cried. She turned to the wall and raised both arms, reaching for the top.

"There isn't time!" I shouted, watching the four guards pick their way through the crowd.

But I bent down and cupped one of her sneakers in my hands—and lifted.

Her hands grazed the top of the wall. "Oh!" she cried out as her sneaker slipped out of my hands and she dropped back to the ground.

"Hold your horses!" one of the dark-uniformed guards cried. "Don't try to run!"

We were caught.

I let out a long sigh and waited for them to circle us.

But as they came running across the crowded walkway, I saw a frantic-looking man and woman step up and block their path.

"Our baby!" the woman cried.

"Have you seen a baby?" the man asked. "A little one?"

"She was in a carriage," the woman added in a trembling voice.

The guards were forced to stop. I bent quickly, grabbed Ashley's sneaker again, and with a loud groan boosted her up to the top of the wall.

Then I leaped as high as I could, grabbed the top, and scrambled over.

"Ow!" I scraped both knees again as I slid down the other side.

I glanced up. We were back in the small park where the barbershop quartet had been singing. The concert music must have ended. The park was nearly deserted.

Ashley was already on her feet and running. Ignoring my throbbing knees, I started after her—and bumped into someone.

We both cried out in surprise.

It was a boy. About our age. Twelve, maybe thirteen.

He had wavy brown hair that looked like it hadn't been brushed in years. He was sort of shabby.

His red- and blue-striped T-shirt was faded and stained, and one sleeve was torn. His wide brown pants stopped just below his knees.

"Watch where you're going!" he cried angrily, rubbing his side.

"Sorry," I murmured. "I was running and—"

"Can you help us?" Ashley asked breathlessly, appearing behind me. "We've got to hide."

"How can you hide in those strange clothes?" the boy asked, pointing at Ashley's Day-Glo shorts. "Are you a circus act or something?"

"No. We—uh— I mean—" I stammered.

"We don't have time to explain," Ashley said impatiently. "Do you know a good place to hide?"

The boy tossed back his brown hair. He stared from Ashley to me. "First, let's get you some real duds," he said.

"Some real *what?*" I demanded.

"You know. Duds. Clothes," he replied, eyeing me curiously. "Where are you from, anyway?"

"Pretty far from here," I told him.

Ashley's eyes were on the wall. The guards would be climbing after us any second. "Please—let's get moving," she pleaded.

"Okay. Follow me," the boy said. He began to trot across the grass.

We followed him out of the small park onto the crowded walkway that led back to the carnival area. "By the way, my name is Paul," he said.

We told him our names. Our eyes were darting over the crowd, searching for guards. Each time we turned a corner, I expected to be grabbed.

The wind swirled and gusted. It blew a woman's wide-brimmed hat into a small fishpond. She started yelling at her husband to wade in and pull it out for her. He didn't seem too happy about the idea.

Ashley and I tried to stay in the shadows as we followed Paul through the park. After what seemed hours, we came to a place called the service area.

Paul led us into a square white-shingled

building. We found ourselves in a musty-smelling room. Paul pointed to several large cardboard cartons against one wall. A sign above the cartons read USED CLOTHING DROP.

"Maybe you can find something that fits," he told us. "Go ahead. Hurry up and change. At least you won't look like freaks!"

Freaks?

Ashley and I hurried over to the cartons, which were piled to the top with old clothing. It was like the stuff you see in antique stores.

Ashley rummaged through a carton and pulled out a long straight brown skirt with a ruffled hem. She pulled it on over her shorts. "Hey, it fits!" she cried happily.

A few seconds later she pulled out a frilly, lacy white blouse. "This is like when I was little," Ashley said, pulling the blouse over her sleeveless T-shirt. "I used to go up to my grandmother's attic and try on her old clothes.

She spun around. "How do I look?"

"Like your grandmother," I told her.

I bent down and tried to find something that would fit me. Paul had his eyes trained on the entrance. Ashley was twirling around in the weird skirt and blouse.

"Why do they have old clothing at an amusement park?" she asked Paul.

"You know. For the unemployed people," Paul replied without turning around. "The park has a lot of services for the poor."

"Really?" Ashley cried, surprised.

"Well, there *is* a Depression going on," Paul replied sharply.

I pulled out a pair of knee-length brown pants like Paul's. And I found a Hawaiian-style sport shirt, all yellow and blue flowers, that might fit okay.

I remembered we read something about the Depression in a history unit. It was a long time ago, when a lot of people were out of work and everyone was poor.

I wanted to ask Paul more about it. But I knew I couldn't. Paul would wonder why I didn't know about it. And I knew there was no way to explain to him about Ashley and me.

I couldn't explain it to myself!

I went into the back room, tugged off my jeans and T-shirt, and pulled on the outfit from the carton. The clothes smelled a little moldy, but they almost fit.

I felt like a real dork with pants that didn't

come all the way down. At least the Hawaiian sport shirt was kind of cool.

How could people wear this stuff? I wondered.

Well, at least it will be easier to keep away from the guards in these clothes, I told myself. As I adjusted the pants, my gaze stopped at my white pump sneakers. Should I trade them in, too?

I had seen a carton of shoes in the other room, big clunky brown and black shoes. Maybe—

"No way!" I cried out loud.

No way was I leaving my pumps behind.

I stepped back into the front room and stretched out my arms. "Hey, Ashley, what do you think?"

My mouth dropped open as I glanced around the room. I let out a startled gasp.

Ashley and Paul were gone.

20

"Hey!"

I stared around the empty room, my heart pounding. "What's the big idea?"

Had Ashley been caught by the guards? Dragged away?

I hurried out the front door—and straight into them both.

Ashley caught the frantic expression on my face. "Paul and I ran out," she explained. "I thought I saw P.D."

"Who is P.D.?" Paul asked.

"We have to find him," Ashley replied breathlessly. "James and I have been searching everywhere for him. We have to find him right away."

A blue-uniformed security guard approached. He was whistling to himself, walking slowly. He stopped whistling when he saw the three of us.

Oh, no, I thought, feeling my stomach tighten with dread. *Caught again?*

I swallowed hard.

The guard started whistling again. He walked right past us.

I realized I'd been holding my breath. I let it out in a long *whoosh.* "These costumes worked!" I exclaimed.

"What does P.D. look like?" Paul asked.

"He's an old man with long white hair and a bushy white beard," Ashley told him. "Sort of like Santa Claus."

"The last time we saw him, he was wearing huge overalls," I added. "Denim overalls. Over a black sweater."

"He shouldn't be too hard to find," Paul replied.

"We *have* to find him," Ashley said, her voice shrill and frightened. "We have to find him or we can't get home."

*   *   *

We searched for a long time. It seemed like hours.

No sign of P.D.

I suddenly realized I was starving. I led Ashley and Paul up to a food stand. A bright electric sign over the counter read CONEY ISLAND DOGS. *Fit For A Millionaire.*

I peered behind the counter to see several hot dogs sizzling on a wide grill. So *that's* what Coney Island dogs are! I told myself.

I turned to Ashley and Paul. "How many do you want? I could eat a dozen!"

"Just one," Ashley said. "With lots of mustard."

Paul lowered his eyes. "None for me," he muttered. "I—uh—don't have any money."

"I'll treat you," I told him. "You helped us get these clothes." I turned to the white-aproned counterman. He wore a tall white chef's hat. "How much are they?" I asked.

"Three cents," he replied in a gruff voice. "How many?"

"Three with lots of mustard," I told him. I turned to Ashley. "If we lived here, we'd be rich!" I exclaimed.

Paul looked puzzled.

"Where we live, hot dogs cost more than a dollar," Ashley explained.

"Stop teasing me," Paul said, smiling. "No one would pay a dollar for a Coney." His smile faded. "Are you really rich?"

I felt all the change in my pockets. I knew I had at least five dollars in my wallet. "We're rich tonight!" I declared.

"Can we go on the Shoot-the-Chute?" Paul asked. "I never have enough money to ride it. Or anything else," he added sadly.

"We have to keep searching for P.D.," Ashley told him.

"But maybe we can do some rides on the way," I said.

As we gobbled down our hot dogs, Paul told us he came to Firelight Park just about every night. He couldn't afford the admission. It cost a dime to get in. So he sneaked in through a hole in the fence back near the woods.

He told us he had four brothers and sisters, and his family lived in a two-room apartment above a dry-cleaning store. "I work during the day, delivering the dry cleaning," Paul said. "I don't get paid a salary. But sometimes the customers give me a few pennies as a tip."

He finished his Coney in about two seconds. I bought him another one. I could tell he was really hungry.

"Of course I give all my money to my family," he continued. "You see, my dad lost his job when the stock market crashed. He goes out every morning, trying to find work. But there are so many men looking for jobs. . . ." His voice trailed off.

I ordered three more Coney Island dogs, and gave the counterman a dime. We gobbled them up quickly. They were really good.

"Let's take Paul on some rides," I whispered to Ashley.

"Okay." She nodded. "I guess we can watch for P.D. on the way."

We made our way through the crowd. The tall torches flickered as we passed, making our shadows dance in front of us.

Paul led the way to a building called The Human Whirlpool. It was really a simple ride. A huge wooden disc stretched across the center of the floor. People crowded onto the disc and sat down. Then the disc began to spin, faster and faster, making everyone tumble and fall all over one another.

We came out laughing, staggering, bumping into one another.

We headed next to a ride called The Air-Flo Dodgem Cars. It was almost like the bumper cars they have at parks today. Except the cars were rounder and taller and didn't move quite as fast.

After the dodgem cars, we were ready for the Shoot-the-Chute. It turned out to be a kind of water-log–roller coaster ride. It was as high as a roller coaster—and everyone had to walk up to the top! No car to carry us up.

Once we got to the top, we climbed into cars that looked like long logs. Then we shot down a watery track, curving to a pond, where we hit with a splash.

"Thank you! That was swell!" Paul declared when we came out. "You two are real pals!" He had a big smile on his face.

That made me feel really good. I'm sure it made Ashley feel good, too.

"What should we do next?" I asked, jingling the change in my pockets.

"I think we should search for P.D.," Ashley

replied. In the flickering torchlight her expression was tense and frightened.

I was having so much fun, I had nearly forgotten about P.D.

The wind suddenly blew hard, a strong, warm gust that fluttered booth awnings and made the trees shake and whisper.

"Hey!" I cried out as an open newspaper flew along the walkway and wrapped itself around my ankles.

As I bent to pull it off me, my eyes fell on the date on the top of the page—and I gasped.

June 15, 1931.

"Ashley—l-look!" I stammered. I shoved the newspaper into her face.

It fluttered and flapped in the wind. She couldn't read it.

"It's June fifteenth!" I cried. "Ashley—it's 1931. Don't you remember?"

Her mouth dropped open. She grabbed the newspaper with both hands and stared at the date on the page.

"The night of the tornado!" I cried.

Stunned, Ashley let go of the newspaper and the wind carried it away. "James—what are we going to do?"

21

"Tornado? What tornado? It's just a little windy," Paul said. He glanced up at the sky that was now starless. "Probably going to rain."

"You don't understand!" Ashley cried shrilly. "There's going to be a tornado! A terrible tornado!"

A slow grin crossed Paul's face. I could see he thought we were joking. "You're pulling my leg, right?"

"No," I told him. "We're serious, Paul. We've got to warn everyone!"

"Everyone has to leave the park!" Ashley cried. "Everyone has to get out!"

"You *mean* it?" Paul demanded, still confused.

The wind was blowing really steadily now. Hats were blowing across the ground. Women grabbed their skirts and held them down. People were laughing, raising their faces to the wind, enjoying the excitement.

Only Ashley and I knew that the excitement would soon turn to terror.

But what could we do? How could we warn everyone?

How could we get everyone out in time?

"Let's tell those two guards!" Ashley cried, pointing to two uniformed men leaning against a white information booth.

She dodged around a group of laughing teenagers who had their arms outstretched and were pretending to fly through the soaring wind. Then she went running to the guards.

Paul and I hurried after her.

"You've got to clear the park—now!" Ashley screamed breathlessly.

The two guards stared at her, their expressions not changing.

"You've got to get everyone out! A tornado is coming!" Ashley cried.

The guards exchanged glances. One of them had a thin blond mustache. His lips twisted into a smile beneath it. "Afraid of a little wind?" he asked in a mocking voice.

Ashley sputtered angrily.

"No—listen to her! She's right!" I stepped in. "It's going to be a terrible tornado. Clear the park! Clear the park!"

The guard with the mustache yawned. "Beat it, kids," he said in a bored voice.

"Go see the sideshow," his partner chimed in. "They've got lots of jokers over there."

"You don't understand!" Ashley shrieked frantically, raising both fists in frustration. "We *know* it's coming! We *know* it's going to destroy the whole park! You've *got* to listen to us! We come from the future!"

Both guards burst out laughing.

"Go have a good time, kids," the mustached guard said, waving us away. "And say hello to Buck Rogers for us!"

"Say hi to Flash Gordon, too!" his partner said, laughing.

Ashley choked out a cry of frustration. She lowered her fists to her sides.

We turned and walked away from the laughing guards.

"Why did you tell him you're from the future?" Paul asked, scratching his long brown hair. "I don't get it. Why do you think a tornado is headed this way?"

"We don't have time to explain," Ashley replied, frowning up at the flickering torches.

"She's right," I said, my eyes searching the long boardwalk. "We've got to find P.D."

"He told us he was here this night, the night of the tornado," Ashley said thoughtfully. "So we've just got to keep looking. We've got to search every inch of the park till we find him."

Suddenly another idea flashed into my mind. "Ashley—maybe the park has a loudspeaker system. You know. For making announcements from the main office."

"Yes!" Ashley cried, her eyes lighting up. "That's a great idea!" She turned excitedly to Paul. "Paul, where's the main office? Can you take us there?"

Paul pointed. "It's that way. Near the front gate. But—"

"We'll tell them to make an announcement!" Ashley cried, hurrying off in the direction Paul had pointed. "They can announce that the park is closed, that everyone has to leave."

"And they can ask P.D. to come to the front gate," I added, trotting after her. "They can call him to the front gate—then he can tell us how to get home!"

It seemed like a good plan. Simple, really.

If it worked, it would save a lot of lives—and get us back to our time.

If it didn't work . . .

Well, I didn't want to think about that.

As the three of us jogged through the crowds to the main office, I was struck by the amazing stillness.

It was so quiet. The air hung heavily over us. So still. Nothing moved. Not a tree leaf trembled.

I felt a cold chill down my back as I realized what it was.

The calm before the storm.

22

A hush seemed to have fallen over the entire park. We ran through the eerie quiet.

Far away, I could hear the sound of the carousel.

The crowd became a blur of smiling faces as we ran. People were gazing up at the sky. It had become a strange yellow gray. As if it had been painted over.

"Hurry!" Ashley cried.

Paul and I were right behind her.

"There it is!" Paul shouted, pointing.

Across a wide plaza stood a long, low red-brick building. The row of windows all along the side was dark.

Breathing hard, we stopped at the double glass doors.

Dark inside. Completely black.

Ashley tugged frantically at one of the doors. It didn't budge. She tried the other one.

Then I noticed the chain tied through the door handles. A brass padlock hung from the chain.

"What do you kids want?" a stern voice called.

All three of us turned to see a tall, lanky guard. He had a long, slender horse face. His blue cap was tilted back on his head, revealing straight, straw-colored hair. His dark eyes were narrowed suspiciously at us.

"We—we have to make an announcement!" I managed to cry.

"We have to get inside! We have to close the park!" Ashley told him in a shrill, desperate voice.

"Office is closed," the guard replied calmly. His long jaw was moving. He was chewing gum, I realized. He motioned toward the dark glass doors. "They all go home at five-thirty. Lucky stiffs."

"But we have to close the park!" Ashley insisted, still clutching the door handles. "We have to warn everyone—"

"Storm's coming up," the guard said, slowly raising his eyes to the sky. "Never saw a sky that yellow. Did you?"

"You don't understand!" Ashley screamed. "It's a tornado! People will be killed! We have to tell them to go home!"

The guard chewed his gum slowly. He stared at Ashley as if he didn't understand a word she was saying.

"It's just going to rain a little," he said finally. "The wind has already stopped."

"No. She's right—" I started. "The tornado—"

But he raised a big, bony-fingered hand to stop me. "Office is closed," he repeated in the same calm voice. "No way to make any kind of announcement."

"Then how can we clear the park?" Ashley cried.

The guard shrugged. "Can't," he said. "Why don't you kids go have some fun?" he suggested, tilting the hat back to scratch his head. "Are your parents around? Maybe you should go find them if you're scared of the storm."

I let out an exasperated sigh. I could see this

guard wasn't going to be any help. We were wasting time—precious time.

The sky had become even stranger, yellow with eerie gray streaks through it. Far in the distance, I thought I could hear the twisting howl of the approaching tornado.

"Ashley, let's go," I murmured, grabbing her arm.

But she pulled away from me and returned to the lanky guard. "Is there any way to call somebody to the gate? Is there any way at all? We need to see a man named P. D. Walters. Is there any way to call for P. D. Walters over the loudspeaker?"

The guard shook his head. "There *is* no loud-speaker," he said. "No way to announce any-thing, as far as I know." His expression hardened. "Run along now, okay? You kids are starting to steam me."

"Come on, Ashley," I pleaded. "We have to go." I pulled her away. We walked halfway across the plaza. Glancing back, I saw the guard leaning against the glass doors, staring at us.

"Why wouldn't he help us?" Ashley de-manded in a high, angry voice. "Why wouldn't he even listen to us? Doesn't he realize what's going to happen? It—it's going to be so horrible, James. And we—we're going to be trapped in it."

"I know," I replied softly, glancing up at the strange yellow sky.

I suddenly realized that Paul hadn't said a word in quite a while. I turned to him and found him staring hard at Ashley and me, a thoughtful look locked on his face.

"Paul—what's wrong?" I asked.

"What name did you just say?" he asked. "Who did you tell the guard you wanted to find?"

"P. D. Walters," Ashley told him. "Remember, Paul? The old man with the white hair and beard? His name is P. D. Walters."

Paul let out a short cry. His mouth dropped open. He stared first at Ashley, then at me. "But that's *impossible!*" he cried.

"What? What's impossible?" I demanded.

"*I'm* P. D. Walters!" Paul exclaimed.

23

Ashley and I both gaped at Paul. Ashley grabbed his arm.

"What do you mean?" she cried shrilly. "What are you saying?"

"*I'm* P. D. Walters!" Paul insisted. An excited laugh escaped from him. "Paul David Walters! That's my name!"

"But you—you—" Ashley stammered, still holding on to him. "You mean that all this time—"

"I don't *believe* it!" I cried, shaking my head. I had to laugh, too. Ashley and I had been such jerks!

We were searching for P.D. as an old man. But we had traveled back *more than sixty years* in time! P.D. was a boy in 1931—not a white-bearded old man!

We had wasted all this time searching for P. D. Walters—when he had been with us the entire night!

"But why are you looking for me? How do you know about me?" P.D. demanded. "I don't understand this. I don't understand any of it at all!"

"We don't either," I confessed.

"We don't have time to talk about it," Ashley said, her eyes raised to the darkening sky. "Just get us back to our time—okay, P.D.?"

"Huh?" His mouth dropped open. "Do *what?*"

"Get us *out* of here," Ashley repeated impatiently. "Send us back to our time."

He stared at her for a long time, thinking very hard. "How would I do that?" he replied finally. His features were tight with confusion. "I'm sorry, Ashley. I really don't know what you mean."

"But you're the only one who can help us!" Ashley screamed. I could hear the panic rise in her voice.

I put a hand on her shoulder, trying to calm her a little. Then I turned to P.D., who was shaking his head fretfully. "Can you show us the way to The Beast?" I asked softly.

"The what?" he replied, more confused than ever.

"Maybe if we found The Beast, we could ride it to the future," I suggested.

"Yes! Good idea!" Ashley cried. "P.D.—hurry! Take us to The Beast!"

"I'm sorry," P.D. replied sadly. "I really am sorry. But I don't know what you're talking about. I've never heard of The Beast."

Ashley let out a long, sad sigh. Her shoulders slumped. "I don't believe this," she murmured. "He can't help us. He can't help us at all."

And just then the wind began to roar.

24

The wind had started as a distant whisper. The whisper was now becoming a steady roar and the trees were beginning to shake. The yellow tint had faded from the sky. The gray quickly darkened to black.

Fire danced in the torches overhead, flickered, then dipped low.

"We're trapped!" Ashley wailed. "Trapped!"

"I'm sorry," P.D. cried, hurrying to keep up with her as she made her way through the crowded boardwalk. "I'm really sorry. I'd help you if I knew what to do."

"Let's find a safe place to hide," I suggested,

shouting over the roar of the wind. "Maybe there's a basement somewhere, or someplace that's protected."

"But we've got to warn people!" Ashley insisted. "We've got to try."

We had wandered back to the carnival area. Up ahead on his small platform, the sideshow barker was still talking into his megaphone, still trying to draw people into his show.

"Ashley, wait!" I cried.

But I was too late. I watched her leap up onto the platform and grab the megaphone out of the startled man's hands. He cried out in protest and stumbled off the platform, landing hard on the concrete.

"Run, everyone!" Ashley shouted into the megaphone. "It's a tornado! Run, everyone! Tornado coming!"

I could barely hear her over the rush of the wind.

"Tornado coming!" she shouted. "Leave the park! Tornado!"

The wind swirled around the sideshow building. People were still heading inside.

I saw two teenagers, their shirts flapping in the strong wind, pointing and laughing at Ashley. A middle-aged man and woman were shaking their heads, probably thinking Ashley was pulling some kind of prank.

The wind was funneled down the midway, flapping awnings, making the flimsy buildings tremble. I heard little kids crying, their frightened wails rising over the rush of the wind.

The sky grew even darker. The swirling air felt hot and wet.

"Tornado! Leave the park! *Please*—listen to me!" Ashley was screaming frantically into the megaphone.

I turned and saw the carnival barker. He was holding his straw hat in one hand to keep it from blowing away. He was talking to two guards. Speaking rapidly, angrily, he was pointing at Ashley.

"Uh-oh!" I cried out loud. "Here come the guards!"

P.D. and I ran up to Ashley. We didn't have to say a word. She saw the guards, too. They were running toward us, their eyes narrowed in anger. The carnival barker hurried after them.

Ashley dropped the megaphone. All three of us began running, running into the wind. It tried to push us back. We lowered our heads and ran harder.

I glanced back. There were *four* guards chasing us now.

"Run!" I screamed. "Keep running!" My words were pushed back in my face by the onrushing wind.

The wind blew so hard, I couldn't breathe. The air was filled with dust, swirling and stinging our faces and lungs.

I closed my eyes and kept running.

When I opened them, I saw we had run up against a tall wooden fence.

"Dead end!" I screamed.

I turned to see the four guards closing in. Their expressions were triumphant when they saw they had us cornered.

I pressed my back against the fence and searched desperately for an escape route. But we were blocked on both sides by big garbage trucks.

The wind howled louder. Louder.

Heads lowered, the guards moved in on us.

We're trapped, I realized, glancing at Ashley and P.D.

They were pressed against the wooden fence,

too. The wind sent Ashley's hair flying wildly about her head.

"Now what?" Ashley cried.

I could barely hear her over the howling wind. The thick dust forced me to shut my eyes again.

We're trapped in the tornado, I realized.

The park is about to be destroyed—and so are we.

25

The guards spread out as they closed in on us. Their angry scowls had turned to eager grins. They knew they had us trapped.

The wind knocked over a large metal trash can and sent it toppling in front of us. I cried out, startled.

Suddenly I felt a tug on my shoulder.

"This way!" P.D. shouted, cupping his hands to be heard over the wind. He started to pull me along the fence.

"Where are we going?" Ashley cried shrilly.

P.D. didn't reply.

We followed him, huddling together, leaning into the wind.

He stopped suddenly—and pushed hard against two wooden fence planks.

They tilted up, and we ducked under them. Escape!

"That's where I sneak into the park!" P.D. cried, grinning. "I knew this fence looked familiar!"

We didn't have time to thank him. All three of us were running full speed now, away from the fence toward the dark woods.

The trees bent low and shook in the raging wind. As we ran toward them, they appeared to come alive, to jump about and dance.

Would we be safer among the trees?

Probably not.

But we didn't stop to think about it. All we could think of was getting away from the guards and hiding until the tornado had passed.

Glancing back, I saw the guards pulling themselves through the fence opening one by one. "Run!" I shouted. "They're coming!"

P.D. slipped and stumbled in the tall grass.

Ashley and I both grabbed him and pulled him to his feet.

We started to run again—then stopped as the enormous shadow loomed over us.

At first I thought it was some kind of gigantic black creature huddled in the trees.

But then my eyes focused on the rising sweep of the tracks as they curved overhead.

"The Beast!"

Ashley and I shouted the words together.

I gaped up at it in disbelief. Had it been standing there the whole time? Could we ride it out of the tornado, out of 1931, back to our time?

I could hear the guards' angry shouts behind us.

Without turning back, we started to run.

A few seconds later we were plunging up the concrete ramp.

"The cars—they're here!" Ashley cried breathlessly.

Yes. As if waiting for us, the empty roller coaster cars stood in the darkness.

Were they already moving?

No. The gusts of wind were making the cars vibrate.

Ashley leaped into the first car. "Hurry!" she screamed.

P.D. had made his way to the controls.

"Pull that lever!" I shouted, pointing. "Pull it down! Then jump on!"

As I climbed in after Ashley, I saw P.D. pull the lever down.

With a hard jolt the car jerked forward. "We're moving!" I cried. The wheels clattered over the track.

"P.D.—hurry!" Ashley screamed.

I twisted back to see why he wasn't joining us.

"No!" I screamed when I saw the two guards grab P.D. and drag him away from the control lever. "P.D.!"

The car was pulling away.

I saw P.D. struggle to free himself. But the two guards held on tight.

"P.D.! P.D.!" Ashley was shouting his name over and over.

He called to us, his voice frightened, desperate.

But he couldn't get away.

Then, just as our car started to pick up speed, I saw two dark figures dive into our car.

The other two guards.

They had leaped into the seat right behind us.

26

I was pressed back against the seat as the car started to climb.

The winds whistled around us, faster, louder.

We're climbing right into the tornado! I thought.

We'll never get out. Never!

The winds will blow us off the track.

And even if we do ride to the end, I realized, the guards are right with us. We haven't escaped at all.

Up, up. The tracks stretched steeper into the raging wind.

And then Ashley and I were both screaming as we plunged straight down.

Down into more wind and darting shadows.

An angry, shrill howl, the howl of the tornado, drowned out our screams.

The car swooped and slid through the wind, through the hot dust, so thick it clogged our throats, through the ceaseless howl.

And then up again. Another steep climb.

And another plunge.

Down into fog. Cooling fog. So wet, so soft against my face.

Had the wind actually stopped howling?

Had we left the tornado behind?

The heavy fog swept over us as we shot forward.

We're riding through clouds, I thought. Soft, cool clouds.

A sharp swerve. Another jarring dip.

I gripped the safety bar, bouncing hard in the seat.

The fog was so heavy, the shadows so thick, I couldn't tell if my eyes were open or shut.

And then suddenly we stopped.

The ride ended in a splash of pale silver moonlight.

I glanced at Ashley. Her face was paler than the light.

We were both breathing hard, still gripping the safety bar.

Finally I managed to pull myself to my feet. I stood and, holding the seat back, stepped out onto the platform.

My legs still rubbery, I helped Ashley out.

The wind had calmed. The moonlight glittered down on us, soft and silvery.

The two guards!

I had nearly forgotten about them.

They had taken the ride with us. They had soared through the darkness, out of the winds, through the shifting, sweeping fog.

We hadn't escaped.

I turned to their seat and prepared to be captured.

"Oh, no!" Ashley screamed shrilly as she saw them.

My mouth dropped open, but no sound came out.

Two gray skeletons sat in the seat behind us, tiny scraps of blue clothing clinging to their bones.

27

The moonlight shone down on the gray-green bones, the black, empty eye sockets, the grinning skulls.

"James—what h-happened?" Ashley stammered, gaping in horror at what remained of the two guards.

"I think we've traveled through time," I told her, unable to take my eyes off the skeletons. "I think we've come back more than sixty years to our own time."

"And the guards?"

"I think they died of old age," I said.

And as I said it, the bones began to crumble.

The patches of blue cloth—what had once been their uniforms—fluttered and floated away in the breeze.

The bones crumbled to gray powder. The powder was carried off by the wind.

"P.D. sent us back in time to 1931," I said, watching the powder float away in the moonlight. "I guess he hoped we could warn people about the tornado and save lives."

"But of course we couldn't," Ashley said sadly. "You can't change history, right? You can't change the past."

"We proved that," I replied thoughtfully. "We didn't change anything at all."

"Are we really back home?" Ashley asked.

I opened my mouth to answer, but a stern voice interrupted.

"How did you kids get back here? What are you doing here?"

Bright flashlights played over our faces, forcing us to cover our eyes.

The Kings Island security guards had finally caught us.

They guided us to the front office and called my mom.

We explained that we had accidentally gotten locked in the park after it closed.

"You should have come right to the security office instead of running around having adventures," a guard scolded, shaking his head.

Ashley and I apologized.

"Can we just go and say good-bye to P.D.?" Ashley asked.

The guard narrowed his eyes at her. "Who?"

"P. D. Walters," Ashley replied. "You know. The old man who tests The Beast at night."

The guards exchanged glances. "Are you feeling okay?" one of them asked her.

"There is no old man who tests The Beast," the other one said, frowning.

We all stared at one another in silence.

Then I asked if Ashley and I could wait for my mom outside.

The guards eyed us suspiciously. "You're not going to run away again?"

"No. Promise," I said.

"Wait by that gate," the guard said, pointing out the window.

Ashley and I wandered outside. The park was dark and silent. Pale moonlight washed over us as we made our way to the front gate.

"The next time they won't catch us," Ashley murmured, grinning.

"Huh? *Next* time?" I cried.

I started to tell her there wouldn't *be* any next time—but something caught my eye.

It was a large brass plaque mounted on the wall beside the gate. The plaque caught the moonlight and glowed brightly against the dark wall.

Ashley saw it, too. We both moved close to read it:

FIRELIGHT PARK

HONOR ROLL

THIS PLAQUE IS IN MEMORIAM

OF THOSE WHO PERISHED

JUNE 15, 1931

My eyes drifted down the long list of names engraved on the metal plaque.

Ashley and I read aloud the very last name at the bottom of the list: "P. D. Walters."

"He didn't get out," Ashley murmured sadly. "He died in the tornado."

"But then, how—"

I never finished my question.

THE BEAST

Through the gate I saw car headlights rolling across the vast parking lot. My mom. Coming to pick us up.

Then behind us I heard a faint sound. A familiar sound, floating on the night air.

I glanced at Ashley. She heard it, too.

We both listened in silence to the sound drifting from the back of the park.

Was it the clatter of roller coaster wheels?

Or was it just the wind?

ABOUT THE AUTHOR

"Where do you get your ideas?"

That's the question that R. L. Stine is asked most often. "I don't know where my ideas come from," he says. "But I do know that I have a lot more scary stories in my mind that I can't wait to write."

So far, he has written nearly three dozen mysteries and thrillers for young people, all of them bestsellers.

Bob grew up in Columbus, Ohio. Today he lives in an apartment near Central Park in New York City with his wife, Jane, and thirteen-year-old son, Matt.

YOU COULD WIN A CHANCE TO RIDE

THE BEAST®

 A MINSTREL® BOOK *Paramount® Parks*  UNITED AIRLINES

One First Prize: Trip for three to Paramount's Kings Island (home of the BEAST®) or the Paramount theme park of the winner's choice.

Four Second Prizes: Four Single-Day Admission Tickets to the Paramount Park near you.

Twenty-Five Third Prizes: An autographed copy of *The Beast*

Name_____Birthdate_____

Address_____

City_____State___Zip_____

Phone (   )_____

POCKET BOOKS *Win a Chance to Ride The Beast*® SWEEPSTAKES
Official Rules:

1) No Purchase Necessary. Enter by submitting the completed Official Entry Form (no copies allowed) or by sending on a 3"x5" card your name and address to the Pocket Books/The Beast Sweepstakes, Advertising and Promotion Department, 13th Floor, 1230 Avenue of the Americas, NY, NY 10020. Entries must be received by 9/30/94. Not responsible for lost, late or misdirected mail. Enter as often as you wish, but one entry per envelope. Winners will be selected at random from all entries received in a drawing to be held on or about 10/3/94.

2) Prizes One First Prize: a weekend for three (the winning minor, one parent or legal guardian and one guest) including round-trip coach airfare from the major U.S. airport nearest the winner's residence served by United Airlines or United Express, ground transportation or car rental, meals and three nights in a hotel (one room, triple occupancy), plus three Weekend (Saturday and Sunday) Admission Tickets to Paramount's Kings Island or the Paramount theme park of the winner' choice (approximate retail value: $3880.26-$3911.70). Winners must be able to travel during the regularly scheduled 1995 operating season of the Paramount Park chosen (approx. 5/5-9/1, 1995). Four Second Prizes: Four Single-Day Admission Tickets to the Paramount Park near you (retail value: $86.84-$107.80). Twenty-Five Third Prizes: An autographed copy of *The Beast* (retail value: $3.99). All dollar amounts are U.S. Dollars.

3) The sweepstakes is open to residents of the U.S. and Canada no older than fourteen as of 9/30/94. Proof of age required to claim prize. Prizes will be awarded to the winner's parent or legal guardian. Void in Puerto Rico and wherever else prohibited by law. Employees of Paramount Communications, Inc., United Airlines and United Express, their suppliers, affiliates, agencies, participating retailers, and their families living in the same household are not eligible.

4) One prize per person or household. Prizes are not tranferable and may not be substituted. All prizes will be awarded. The odds of winning a prize depend upon the number of entries received.

5) If a winner is a Canadian resident, then he/she must correctly answer a skill-based question administered by mail. Any litigation respecting the conduct and awarding of a prize in this publicity contest may be submitted to the Regie des Loteries et Courses du Quebec.

6) All federal, state and local taxes are the responsibility of the winners. Winners will be notified by mail. First Prize winner will be required to execute and return an Affidavit of Eligibility and Release within 15 days of notification or an alternate winner will be selected.

7) Winners grant Pocket Books and Paramount Parks the right to use their names, likenesses, and entries for any advertising, promotion and publicity purposes without furthur compensation to or permission from the entrants, except where prohibited by law.

8) For a list of major prize winners (available after 10/3/94), send a stamped, self-addressed envelope to Prize Winners, Pocket Books/The Beast Sweepstakes, Advertising and Promotion Department, 13th Floor, 1230 Avenue of the Americas, NY, NY 10020. 985